BROOKLYN, NY

Published by POW! a division of powerHouse Packaging & Supply, Inc.

32 Adams Street, Brooklyn, NY 11201-1021

info@powkidsbooks.com www.powkidsbooks.com
www.powerHouseBooks.com www.powerHousePackaging.com

Library of Congress Control Number: 2017940931

ISBN: 978-1-57687-850-7

Printing and binding by Midas Printing, Inc.

Book design: Krzysztof Poluchowicz

10 9 8 7 6 5 4 3 2 1

Printed in China

MAKE A FACE

WRITTEN BY
RICARDO ALEGRIA, JR.

ILLUSTRATED BY
ANYA KUVARZINA

What makes a  ?

Just a
mouth
and two
eyes,
a nose
and
a chin?

Yes, that's all true,
but did you know that

YOUR FACE can MAKE FACES too?

Follow this way,
and let's see
**what your face
can do.**

Make a

FUNNY FACE,

as funny
as can be.

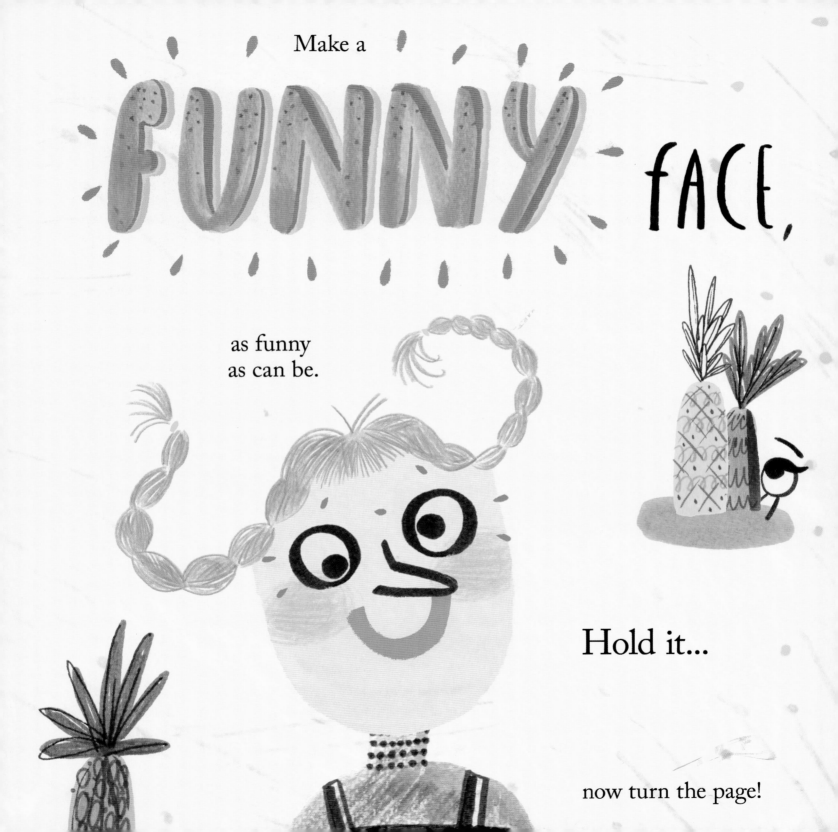

Hold it...

now turn the page!

HAHA hoHO

Look at the FUNNY hippo dancing for you!

Next, make a

SAD
FACE.

Well,
not
too
sad
now.

Turn the page s l o w l y this time.

OH NO!

Look at the SAD llama pout!

Let's get him happy.

Can you make a

HAPPY FACE?

Hooray!

Look at the HAPPY llama prancing about.

Now make a

SERIOUS

face.

OH
ME!
OH MY!

See the
SERIOUS
king lion sitting on his throne.

Time to make a

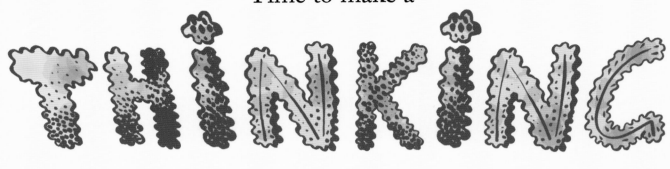

THINKING
FACE.

What is
a thinking face?

Well, what do you
THINK?

Don't forget to turn the page.

Let's not make a peep.

The **wise owl**
in the tree
is deep
in thought.

Are you ready for this?

Make a

FRIGHTENING FACE.

then carefully turn the page.

HOW ABOUT THAT !

A BIG elephant is frightened...

Let's pick up the pace.

Make a PLAYFUL face

...of a little mouse!

and **quickly** turn the page.

Make a face like a MONKEY and swing your arms about.

You've got the hang of it!

Look at

all the

curious

monkeys

swinging

limb to limb!

Something **different** now…

Wink your Left Eye, then wink your Right Eye.

Now wink

BOTH eyes TEN times.

That's it!

Whee!

Twinkle, Twinkle, TEN happy little STARS

blinking back at you.

How about a

SNEEZY

FACE?

TRY
WIGGLING

YOUR
nose

without
using
your
hands.

That's not so easy to do!

Do you sometimes feel shy?

Let's try a BASHFUL face,

and turn the page gently this time.

Look at the

BASHFUL

turtle and snail,

tucked inside
their shells.

Oh,
I'm
getting
tired.

Can
you
make
a
SLEEPY
fACE ?

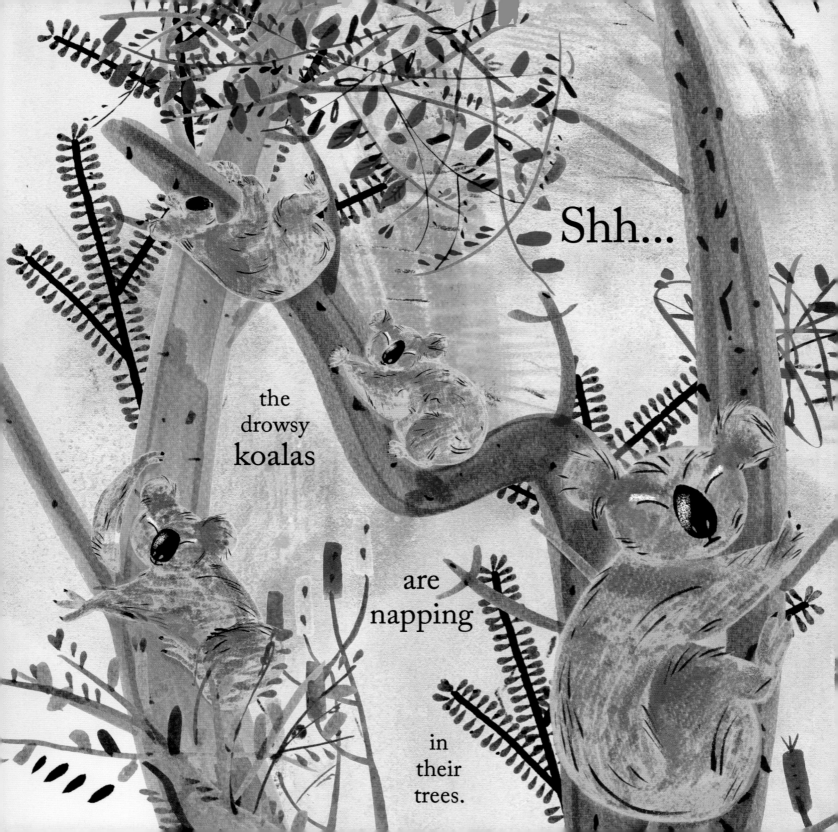

Shh...

the
drowsy
koalas

are
napping

in
their
trees.

Boo boo boo!

This book is almost over.

That was so **SUPER fUN!**

I say we go through it
again.

Shall we give it
another run?

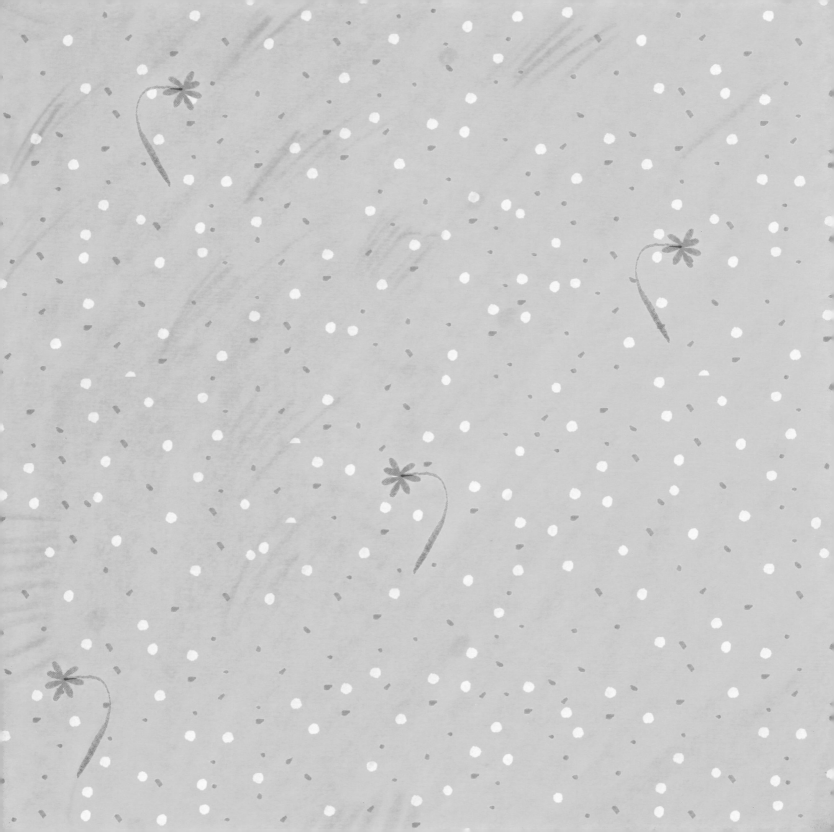